E   Bailey, Jill
B   Save the Macaws

DECLARATION

•

I hereby declare that
all the paper produced
by Cartiere del Garda S.p.A.
in its Riva del Garda mill
is manufactured completely
<u>Acid-free and Wood-free</u>

Dr. Alois Lueftinger
Managing Director and General Manager
Cartiere del Garda S.p.A.

Earth's Endangered Creatures

SAVE THE MACAWS

Written by
Jill Bailey

Illustrated by
Ann Baum

STECK-VAUGHN
LIBRARY
A Division of Steck-Vaughn Company

Austin, Texas

This series is concerned with the world's endangered animals, the reasons why their numbers are diminishing, and the efforts being made to save them from extinction. The author has described these events through the eyes of fictional characters. Although the situations are based on fact, the people and the events described are fictitious.

Editor: Andy Charman
Designer: Mike Jolley
Picture researcher: Jenny Faithful
Consultant: Peter Evans

Library of Congress Cataloging-in-Publication Data

Bailey, Jill.
Save the macaws / written by Jill Bailey :
illustrated by Ann Baum
p. cm. — (Save our species)
Includes index.
Summary: Hector observes a pair of blue-and-gold macaws in the wild and explains their mating habits to two visiting students. Similiar fictional vignettes combined with factual information focus on the behavior and endangered situation of the macaw.
ISBN 0-8114-2712-9
1. Macaws—Juvenile fiction. [1. Macaws—Fiction.]
I. Baum, Ann, ill. II. Title. III. Series: Bailey, Jill. Save our species.
PZ10.3.B155Sam   1992   91-19871
[Fic]—dc20   CIP AC

Color separations by Positive Colour Ltd, Maldon, Essex, Great Britain.
Printed and bound by L.E.G.O., Vicenza, Italy

1 2 3 4 5 6 7 8 9 0 LE 96 95 94 93 92

CONTENTS

MACAWS
AT HOME

There was a sudden rustle of wings and the nearby branches shook. **Hector Hernandez** froze, and turned his head slowly. A pair of red-and-green macaws had landed in a tree about 20 feet away. Their brilliant plumage glowed in the sunlight filtering down into the Peruvian rain forest. Hector could hear nuts being broken. Slowly, he lifted the insect-proof netting away

A blue-and-gold macaw in its forest home. This forest is being cut down to make room for human dwellings.

from his face and raised his binoculars. The macaws were feeding, gripping nuts in one claw while they cracked them with their powerful bills.

The macaws finished their snack, and began to preen each other. Male and female macaws pair for life, and spend a lot of time preening each other's feathers. When birds preen they use their bills to clean and arrange their feathers.

Hector forced himself to turn back to the birds he was really here to watch — a pair of blue-and-gold macaws that were nesting in a tree trunk below him. Macaws nest in ready-made holes. He could just make out the bright blue head of the female as she sat on her eggs.

Soon the male returned, his throat swollen with food for his mate. Macaws and many other parrots have a large pouch, or crop, in their throats, which they use to store food. The male coughed up, or regurgitated, the food for the female to swallow.

From his harness up in a tree, Hector could see across the top of the forest. The netting with which his face was covered protected him from biting insects.

There was a crackle from the walkie-talkie radio strapped to Hector's waist. It was Pedro, a Brazilian researcher.

"Hector," said Pedro, "We're going to stop for lunch now."

Hector was glad to climb down for lunch. He raised his insect net and dozens of tiny stingless bees, attracted by his sweat, crawled over his face.

"The female macaw is sitting on eggs," he told Pedro and Veronica. Veronica was a visiting student studying the breeding problems of macaws.

"Is this one of the best places for them to breed?" she asked.

"Yes," said Hector. "There are plenty of large, old trees and no people – except us! The big, old trees are gone from so many places. Still, macaws don't seem to do that well here. A study of 100 nesting pairs showed that only 15 to 25 young were raised

A pair of blue-and-gold macaws at their nest hole. The female does not need to be camouflaged, because she cannot be seen by predators when she is in the hole.

in this park each year. Only a few of the birds that live here seem to nest in any one year.

"These blue-and-gold macaws had a bad time last year. The female was driven out of her nest hole by another pair, and the male vanished. We think he was

Macaws fly through the forest in small groups, calling noisily. They can be heard from a long way off.

killed. Now she has a new mate. Even where there are lots of holes, only one or two pairs nest in every 2 square miles."

The Manu National Park is a dense rain forest like that shown above. Rivers wind between the trees. The green canopy is broken here and there by an extra tall tree that pushes into the sunlight.

"There are seven species of macaws in this national park," Hector went on proudly. "We are trying to find out how many of each kind there are, what they eat, and how and where they find food. We know that scarlet macaws eat over 40 different kinds of nuts and fruits.

"We don't really know much about how wild macaws live. Some may move to different parts of the forest at different times of the year. We need to learn much more if we are to save them from extinction."

After lunch, the researchers set off along the forest trail. They were following a map and looking for signs of macaws. Macaws waste a lot of food. They like to take nuts back to a perch to eat, but often they accidentally drop them. The shells and husks of the nuts they do eat also fall to the ground. Nuts cracked by macaws have incredibly smooth cuts. The shell often shows grooves where the bird has gripped it in its bill. This makes it easy to tell whether macaws or monkeys have dropped the shells.

They were counting shells beneath a large nut tree when Veronica gave a cry. She had found the tracks of an ocelot and they looked fresh.

Ocelots will stalk macaws when the birds are feeding on the ground. Danger also comes from the air; large forest eagles can easily seize a perching macaw.

Veronica knelt down and examined the seeds that they had found beneath the tree.

"Some of these are very poisonous," she remarked. "These are soapbox tree seeds, and those are mahogany seeds."

"Macaws seem to be able to cope with the poisons," said Hector. "They also eat unripe fruit, which other animals cannot eat. They can eat food that no other animals want."

"How can they eat poison?" asked Veronica.

"Macaws regularly visit clay

Each macaw has its own characteristic pattern of lines on its face. This is how researchers recognize individual birds.

licks," replied Hector. "These are banks of clay that have been exposed by the river. The birds swallow chunks of clay. We think clay helps to absorb the poisons, or to make them harmless. The natives of the Andes mix wild potatoes with clay to remove the poisons."

"I'd like to see the macaws on the clay," said Veronica.

"We'll go tomorrow morning," promised Hector.

At dawn, they set out for the clay lick. It was a steep bank beside a gurgling stream. Pedro and Hector flung a rope over the branches of a tree nearby, and hauled up a rope ladder. Now it was Pedro's turn to keep watch above. He was to watch the birds flying in from other parts of the forest, and to note where each group came from.

Hector and Veronica settled down with notebooks. It was a good chance for Veronica to learn to recognize individual macaws and parrots.

Macaws and other forest parrots visit clay licks like the one shown here about three times a week.

Soon the researchers heard birds screeching. Small groups of parrots flew in and started squabbling over the best places on the bank. Clinging on with their claws, the parrots scraped chunks of clay into their mouths with their bills. Crumbs spilled into the stream. Soon the bank was thick with hundreds of colorful parrots. With them were a few species of medium-sized macaws. Chestnut-fronted macaws and red-bellied macaws were feeding side by side.

Pedro radioed down from his lookout post. "Large macaws flying in from the west – I think they're scarlets."

The large macaws began to arrive in twos and threes. At first they were cautious, sitting in trees, preening nervously, screeching and squabbling. Soon they, too, flew onto the bank.

Veronica and Hector were making notes and sketching the birds as quickly as they could.

All of a sudden, there was a lot of noise and wing-flapping, and the birds began flying away. A shadow darkened the bank, and there was an anguished squawk. A harpy eagle had snatched an unlucky parrot.

"Time to go," said Hector. "They won't come back now, the sun is too high."

Hector was eager to get back to camp. He and Pedro were due to leave that afternoon to visit a research project in Brazil. They were hoping to see the rare hyacinth macaws.

Below: *Harpy eagles are fierce predators. With their powerful talons, they can easily capture macaws and even monkeys.*

Above: *Scarlet macaws and red-and-green macaws on a clay lick in Peru. This area is home to seven species of macaws.*

The following day, Hector and Pedro were in the grasslands of southeast Brazil, the home of the hyacinth macaw. Pedro led Hector to a small, swampy area surrounded by palm trees.

"Is this where they nest?" asked Hector.

"It is," replied Pedro. "We'll probably find the macaws near the cattle. Cattle feed on palm nuts, and macaws do, too."

As they approached the cattle, Pedro spotted a large, dark

Butia palm trees in Brazil. Hyacinth macaws nest in palm trees in woodland bordering the rivers, or in holes in nearby cliffs.

macaw sitting on a fence post. It was watching some others hunt for nuts on the ground.

The birds noticed the men and flew off, squawking loudly. Their brilliant purple plumage gleamed in the afternoon sun.

"Has the pet bird trade hurt their numbers?" asked Hector.

"Yes," replied Pedro. "Cattle ranchers are also moving their cattle into this area. Hyacinth macaws make very good pets. Not only are they extremely beautiful, but they are easily tamed and very good-tempered. They are also good talkers.

"Of course, to get good pets you have to get them used to humans while they are young. That is why trappers try to take the young from the nests. Then this kind of thing happens."

Pedro showed Hector a palm tree that had been broken off, leaving a jagged stump.

"There was a nest with two chicks in here before I went to Peru," he said. "Trappers must have cut the whole tree down. That's another nest site lost."

The hyacinth macaw is the largest species. Only about 3,000 remain in the wild because so many have been taken for the pet trade and for bird collectors.

"Can't you stop the trapping?" asked Hector.

"It is already illegal," Pedro said. "However, it makes the local people a lot of money. One of these birds can bring up to $22,000 abroad. The trappers are paid very little, but even that is more than they are paid for other kinds of work. Sadly, some smugglers don't look after the birds. For every macaw that arrives safely abroad, five probably die on the way."

Pedro and Hector visited a local trapper, Felipe. Hector was upset to see the children's ragged clothes, the dirty streets, and small, dark shacks with no water or electricity. Felipe was griping about the broken tree.

"The people who broke that tree weren't local ones," he said. "We don't cut trees down. We want the birds to keep nesting here. We just climb up and take the chicks. Of course, we always leave one chick in the nest so that the parents will stay. If we didn't do that, there wouldn't be more birds for the future."

Felipe's wife, Conchita, was feeding some young macaw chicks with a spoon. Hector was relieved to see how much these trappers cared for the young birds. He

A pair of hyacinth macaws at their nest. The trees that these macaws nest in are often cut down by cattle ranchers.

knew, however, that many birds would die after they left the safety of Felipe's home.

"Do you have any idea who cut that tree?" Pedro asked.

"No," said Felipe, "but a man and a boy have been asking for food and shelter in Salinas. That's the next village."

Pedro was angry.

"I'm going to track them down and contact the police," he said firmly. "Once these people find a nesting area, they won't stop at just one visit."

Conchita fed the macaw chicks on a diet of gooey cereal, cornmeal, and boiled rice.

THEFT IN THE JUNGLE

Carlos Silva looked glumly at the rain; it ran off the tin roofs and trickled down the dirty street. Gray skies stretched over São Paulo, the huge, sprawling city in southeast Brazil. Carlos and his family had come to this dreary shantytown a year ago.

Carlos looked around at the litter, the mangy dog scavenging behind the shack, and the thin, pale children playing in the mud. He wished he was back in the forest. There the rain sang as it trickled through the trees and the birds answered it.

There were no birds here, not even his pet macaw, Coco. Coco had fled when the ranchers had come with their guns and forced Carlos's family out of their home. The ranchers wanted their land to raise cattle. His family had come to São Paulo with just a few possessions.

Carlos's father had found work as a laborer, but then he had become ill. Now they relied on the little money Carlos's mother earned selling baskets.

It was a good thing Coco had not come with them. There was no food to spare, and no money to buy grain. Carlos hoped the bird had survived in the forest.

Tomorrow would be better. Uncle Emilio was coming.

Left: *Carlos was unhappy. He missed the jungle's singing birds and bright flowers, and he missed collecting fruit and going fishing.*

Above: *The rain forest in Brazil. Carlos's family had been able to grow food and keep a cow. In São Paulo, they had little to eat.*

Uncle Emilio's arrival made everyone happy. He'd brought a big basket of fruit for Carlos's mother, and cola for his father. Emilio ran a small pet shop in Rio de Janeiro. Carlos loved to visit him and see all the animals, especially the parrots. They reminded him of Coco.

Uncle Emilio wanted to take Carlos on a trip back to the forest. He was going to catch parrots for his shop, he said.

"Ordinary parrots, or special ones to sell?" asked Carlos's father. He knew that his brother sometimes sold rare parrots for lots of money to foreign dealers. The dealers would then smuggle the birds out of the country.

"Special ones," smiled Emilio. "I need Carlos's help because he is young and very good at climbing trees. I'll give him a share of the money we make."

Carlos was excited. It would be the first time he'd see the forest since they had left for the city. He felt proud that he could earn some money for his family.

Uncle Emilio in his pet shop. Emilio caught macaws illegally and sold them to foreign dealers.

A hyacinth macaw bred in captivity. People should never buy macaws that have been taken from the wild. Birds bred in captivity make happier pets.

"What kind of birds are we collecting?" Carlos asked.

"Hyacinth macaws," he said.

"I've never seen any," Carlos said. "Are they in the forest?"

"There weren't any where you lived," explained Emilio. "They live in open country. We're not going to real rain forest, but to small areas of woods and palm groves." Emilio showed Carlos a photo of hyacinth macaws.

Three days later, they were camped in the Salinas grassland.

Carlos and Emilio set out just after dawn. A group of macaws flew past them, shrieking loudly. Carlos had never seen such big ones. They looked almost black against the dawn sky.

"In the sunshine," said Emilio, "the colors are magnificent."

Emilio led Carlos to a clump of palm trees. As they advanced, a hyacinth macaw flew out of a tree, squawking angrily.

"That looks like a nest hole," said Emilio. "Why don't you climb up and have a look?"

Carlos began to climb up. When he was a short way from the nest, the female bird flew out, surprising him. He lost his balance and fell out of the tree. Carlos grabbed at a branch, but it bent under him, and he fell about 15 feet to the ground.

"I've hurt my ankle," he groaned, trying to stand.

Emilio bound Carlos's ankle with his scarf.

"Never mind," said Emilio. "We'll cut the tree down." He'd brought a small chain saw with him. The sound echoed across the terrain. Carlos was horrified as the tree crashed down.

"Won't it hurt the babies?" Carlos asked, as he felt gently in the hole for the chicks. To his relief, the first chick he brought out seemed fine. It bobbed its head and chirped. The second wasn't fine. It was lying in a strange, twisted position, still and lifeless.

"Let's go," said Emilio. "Someone may have heard us."

As Carlos reached the hole, the female macaw flew out. Carlos was so startled that he fell. Now they would cut down the tree.

Carlos and Emilio returned to camp. Carlos had brought some grain for the birds, but he had not expected such a tiny chick.

"It hardly has any feathers," he said. "Do you think it will survive? It can't eat this grain. It needs something softer."

"We'd better buy some rice and cereal then," said Emilio.

They left for Salinas. Carlos was carrying the chick, hidden under a cloth in his basket. As they looked in the window of a village shop, Carlos noticed two men watching them closely. He nudged his uncle. Emilio quickly went inside the shop and bought some grain.

An adult scarlet macaw and chicks at the nest hole. A female macaw feeds her young on food that she has already partially digested.

The two men moved even closer. It was Hector and Pedro. Just then, the chick started chirping.

"What's that noise?" Pedro asked, though he already knew.

Carlos slowly lifted the cloth.

"Come on," said Emilio, urgently, "We have to go."

Emilio started to walk away. Just then, a local policeman arrived. He had come to arrest Emilio. He searched Emilio's bag and found the saw with fragments of palm leaves still clinging to it. The policeman told Emilio that he had to go to the police station. The two men turned to walk away.

"I can't jail the boy – he's too young," said the policeman.

"We'll take him back to our village," said Pedro. "Felipe and Conchita will look after him."

Soon, Felipe and Conchita were showing Carlos how to make a good meal for his chick.

A young Jivaro native wearing a ceremonial headdress made from macaw and parrot feathers. His people have hunted macaws for their feathers for centuries.

"Do you realize that this chick will probably die," said Pedro sternly, "even if it survives the trip to São Paulo?"

Carlos looked up miserably.

"In a few years," Pedro went on, "there won't be any more hyacinth macaws left because so many have been taken. Other kinds are already extinct."

Carlos was shocked to think that such beautiful birds might

Hahn's macaws are bred and kept in captivity. If enough birds are kept for breeding instead of being sold as pets, there would be no need to trap wild birds.

disappear completely.

"Then I'll keep this one," he said. "Uncle Emilio is in jail; he can't stop me. I won't let it die."

Felipe watched the boy. Felipe saw that he cared for the chick.

"You can stay with us as long as you like," Felipe said. "We'll show you how to feed the chick and look after it properly."

Hector and Pedro went home.

"Why don't you tell the police about Felipe?" asked Hector.

"I need to do research here," said Pedro, "I don't want to upset the local people. At least they are careful not to take too many birds, or to damage their nest holes. It's better to teach the locals to care about the birds.

Perhaps one day tourists will want to come and see the birds. That would bring money into the area, and people wouldn't need to sell macaws."

Wild hyacinth macaws face many threats. Their nest trees are destroyed by ranchers, and they are hunted for food and feathers and for the pet trade.

FOR LOVE OF MACAWS

Arthur Copland held out his hand with some nuts and seeds.

"Pepe eat! Pepe eat! Come and get it!" called the macaw.

Pepe, a large scarlet macaw, landed on his shoulder and nuzzled Arthur. Then Pepe bent down to look at her breakfast. Ignoring all the colorful seeds, she chose the largest Brazil nut and flapped back to her perch, making small noises.

Pepe and Arthur were good friends. Pet macaws need lots of attention. They often form long-lasting relationships with humans.

Pepe held the nut firmly with her claw, and pressed the shell with the points of her beak. Then she put it between her two bills, or mandibles, and gripped it firmly. Once it cracked, Pepe used her tongue to take the nut from its shell.

Pepe had been Arthur's main companion since his wife had died forty years ago. The parrot had been wrongly named. A bird

Scarlet macaws preening. This keeps the birds clean, for it gets rid of parasites and the bases of dead feathers that cause disease.

breeder had offered to find out Pepe's sex, and they had found that Pepe was a female! The bird was now at least forty-five years old. Pepe had won many prizes in bird shows, but lately Arthur had left her home.

The next day, Arthur was at a bird show when his friend, Bill Baker, walked in with a man.

"Arthur," said Bill, "meet Clifford Sykes, chief keeper at the Parrot Park." That was a bird zoo that specialized in breeding parrots and macaws.

"I've been wanting to meet you," said Cliff. "I hear you have a female scarlet macaw. We were hoping you'd lend her to us to

Scarlet macaws in flight. This species is common in captivity but endangered in the wild.

see if we can breed her. There is a great shortage of female scarlet macaws."

Arthur didn't like the idea.

"I'm not sure about that," he said slowly. "Pepe has been with me for so long. I'd be lost without her! "

"Do you know that the scarlet macaw is now an endangered species?" Clifford asked.

"I had no idea," said Arthur. "I thought they were common."

"They are, in captivity," said Cliff, "but the rain forest is being cut down quickly, and many macaws are being captured for the pet bird trade.

"They are already extinct in much of Central and South America. That's why we need to breed them. We need lots of birds in captivity in case the wild birds disappear completely. If we can also provide enough birds for the pet trade, maybe we can persuade people not to buy birds that have been caught in the wild. We still have a lot of work to do in that area."

Macaws are sociable birds. It is not kind to keep them alone. Macaw pairs are affectionate.

Arthur wanted to help, but he just couldn't bring himself to part with Pepe.

"Perhaps you'd like to come up to the Parrot Park one day," suggested Clifford, "and see our breeding birds."

When Arthur got home, he was greeted by loud squawks. "Hello Arthur! Tea now!" said the bird. As Arthur boiled the water, Pepe suddenly began to squawk an alarm. There was someone at the front door.

Arthur peered out to see who the visitor was. The face seemed familiar, and then Arthur realized it was a man who had been standing near him while he was talking to Clifford and Bill. He opened the door cautiously.

"Good afternoon," said the stranger. "I'm Trevor Hughes. I'm a bird dealer, and I'd very much like to buy your macaw."

"How did you know I had one?" asked Arthur.

"I could hear it from the road," said the man. Arthur thought it was more likely that the man had overheard his earlier conversation with Cliff.

"Sorry," said Arthur, firmly. "The bird is not for sale." He accompanied the stranger to the gate to make sure that he didn't hang around.

Arthur was afraid that the stranger might attempt to steal Pepe. Macaws are often stolen because they are so valuable.

Arthur didn't trust Trevor Hughes too close to his beloved Pepe. He knew that in many places it was illegal to send these macaws to another country or to receive them. So there might soon be a shortage of scarlet macaws in some countries. Then a dishonest dealer could make a lot of money selling these birds.

Right: *An illegal bird market.* Below: *A bird market in Hong Kong. Hundreds of thousands of birds are sold every year. It is less costly to get birds from the wild than to breed them in captivity.*

After the parrot show, Cliff Sykes went to a conference in the Philippines. While he was there, he visited a bird dealer who had two Spix's macaws. These could be the rarest of all macaws. There is likely only one left in the wild, and about 25 in captivity, most of them old.

It is difficult to find out where the birds are. Spix's macaws have been protected by law for so long that most privately-owned birds have been caught illegally. The only hope for saving the species is to breed them in captivity, then release some of them in the wild – if a safe enough place can be found.

A Lear's or indigo macaw. There have never been many of this species. They have lost much of their habitat, and too many have been collected for the trade in caged birds.

Clifford wanted to borrow the birds to breed them. The man didn't want to part with them.

"They won't breed," he said. "I've had them for years."

"Perhaps," said Cliff, "they're the same sex. Do you know if they are male or female?"

"No," said the dealer, firmly. "The operation they use to find out is too risky. These birds are too valuable for that."

"There is a new method being developed," said Clifford. "They take one of the feather sheaths and test it. It's very safe."

"No thanks," said the dealer. "If you want to buy the birds, I'll accept $35,000 each."

"We don't have the funds," said Clifford, angrily.

Cliff returned home. He was angry with the dealer for being so greedy. The dealer knew that the fewer Spix's macaws there were, the more valuable his would be. He wasn't interested in helping a breeding program.

A pair of Spix's macaws, the rarest of all macaws. There is only one left in the wild. Captive birds are very valuable.

Arthur went to see Clifford at the Parrot Park as planned. Many of the macaws were flying outside in a very large aviary.

"These birds usually breed at this time of year," explained Cliff. "Although macaws pair for life, they can be very choosy about their mates, and they breed best with a partner they really like. So we give them the chance to meet up and choose."

"That's an odd pair," noted Arthur, seeing birds of different colors preening each other.

"Yes," said Clifford. "That's a male scarlet macaw and a female blue-and-gold. The male looks as if he may mate with her. See how his cheeks blush? They will produce hybrid young, a mix of the two color patterns. However, we would prefer the birds to produce more of their own species. Hybrids are popular in the U.S., but not in Europe. We thought Pepe might be a better mate for him."

On a table Arthur saw a pile of brilliant feathers.

"We save feathers when they drop out," said Cliff. "We send them to Central America. The local people use them in ritual dances. A lot of macaws are killed for their feathers. By sending the feathers so they can be sold or rented, we hope to keep the wild birds alive."

Cliff and Arthur moved into the breeding section of the zoo. In one room, baby macaws were being reared by hand.

Different species of macaws may breed together in captivity to produce hybrid young.

A macaw in a zoo. Macaws reared in captivity are calmer and more affectionate than wild ones.

Arthur was fascinated by the tiny macaws. Some had hardly any feathers, while some had a few spiky adult feathers just beginning to show.

"What are these?" he asked.

"Military macaws," said Cliff. "That one's six weeks old."

"There's a sick one," said Arthur, pointing to one of them.

"No, it's not," laughed Cliff. "That one just ate. The lump you see is a crop, a throat pouch for storing food. Digestion takes a while because seeds are very hard. The macaw also has a muscular gizzard. This often contains grit, which helps to break down the seeds."

"Macaws breed slowly," said Cliff. "They produce only two eggs a year, which do not always hatch. If we remove the eggs and rear the young ourselves, the adults will usually lay again the same year. That way we get twice as many eggs. Also, birds we rear ourselves are more likely to live than the others."

In the next room were some macaws with chicks.

"We always let the birds raise some of their own chicks," said Cliff. "After all, one day we may want to reintroduce them to the wild, and they need to have the experience. We've found that it also makes them happier."

"Is it true that birds bred in captivity are more healthy than wild ones?" asked Arthur.

"Usually," replied Cliff. "Wild birds often have parasites and diseases. Birds caught for the pet trade also catch diseases from other birds while they are being transported."

Baby chicks are helpless at birth, and have only a few fluffy feathers. From left to right, the picture below shows chicks at 8 to 9 weeks, 4 weeks, 6 weeks, and at 11 to 12 weeks.

"Do you ever sell these young birds as pets?" asked Arthur.

"Very seldom," replied Cliff. "We keep most of them so that we can build up a large captive population. In any case, macaws are not really very easy to care for as pets. They are sociable birds, and if they are left alone they can become very bad-tempered. They can give a nasty bite and their claws are sharp, too. They need at least two hours of human attention a day to be happy. They're also noisy.

"Macaws can live as long as humans, but only if they are well cared for. Unhappy birds suffer from stress. The stress makes them more likely to catch diseases."

"I wonder if Pepe is stressed out," said Arthur.

"How long have you had her?" asked Cliff.

"Forty years," said Arthur. "I traveled to South America on a cargo ship, and I bought her in a market. She was being so badly treated by the man who owned her that I had to rescue her!"

"In that case," said Cliff, "she must be well over forty years old. I doubt she will breed at that age, and it would certainly upset her to move. It would be best if you keep her."

Arthur returned home to the usual warm welcome from Pepe. He tickled the bird's head affectionately. He had never realized that he had taken the place of a lifelong mate for Pepe, just as Pepe had helped to comfort him over the loss of his wife all those years ago.

Left: *Arthur returned to Pepe. Like all macaws, Pepe was very smart and easily bored. People should know this before deciding on a macaw or a parrot for a pet.*

Above: *A military macaw in its natural home, a South American mountain forest. If it is to survive, the forest must be preserved and trade in wild birds must end.*

MACAW

UPDATE

Macaws are large, intelligent parrots that live in rain forests and other wooded areas of tropical and subtropical Central and South America. There are 16 different species. The macaw population in the wild is falling drastically. The main threats are the destruction of their habitats, and capture for trade to supply pet shops and collectors. This is happening even though capture and export of wild macaws is illegal in many countries. Many macaws die before they reach their destination. As a species becomes rarer, it is sold illegally for large sums of money. As its value increases, more birds are stolen from the wild.

Blue-and-gold Macaw ● This species is up to 35 inches long, and has a very long tail. It is quite common in lowland South America and Panama, especially in riverside forests and palm swamps. It has suffered from habitat loss, and large numbers have been trapped for the bird trade. It breeds well in captivity.

Chestnut-fronted Macaw ● This species is sometimes called the severe macaw and is only about 19 inches long. It is still common in open lowland forests throughout northern South America, but it has disappeared from many areas recently. It is rare in captivity.

Hyacinth Macaw ● This is the largest species and grows up to 40 inches long. It lives in riverside forests and palm swamps of southern Brazil, eastern Bolivia, and northeastern Paraguay. It is uncommon and very valuable. There are only a few in captivity. The main threat has been trapping for the bird trade.

Blue-and-gold Macaw

Chestnut-fronted Macaw

Hyacinth Macaw

Lear's Macaw ● This species grows to a length of about 29 inches. It is found in canyon country with thorn scrub and clumps of palms in northeastern Brazil. There have never been many Lear's macaws. Today there may be only about 20 birds left. Its habitat is being destroyed by cattle ranchers.

Red-bellied Macaw ● This species is only 18 inches long. It is found in palm swamps in northern South America. Its survival depends on the survival of the palm swamps. It is very nervous, and does not breed easily in captivity.

Lear's Macaw

Spix's Macaw

Red-bellied Macaw

Red-and-green Macaw

Scarlet Macaw

Military Macaw

Red-and-green Macaw ● Sometimes known as the green-winged macaw, this species grows up to 35 inches long. It is found in lowland forests in tropical and subtropical Central and South America, but its forest home is being destroyed. Only a few have bred in captivity.

Spix's Macaw ● This species grows to a length of only 22 inches. It is found in palm groves in northeastern Brazil. It was probably never very numerous, but because of trapping for the bird trade it is now extremely rare. There may be only one bird left in the wild and about 25 in captivity worldwide.

Scarlet Macaw ● This species grows up to 35 inches long. It is widespread in the lowlands of South and Central America, where it prefers to live in open woodland, trees along rivers, grasslands, and plantations. It is threatened by destruction of its habitat, illegal trapping for the pet trade, and killing for its feathers. It breeds well in captivity.

Military Macaw ● This species grows to about 29 inches long. It is found in mountain forests of Central and South America. It is threatened by habitat destruction, illegal trapping for the bird trade, and killing for the feather trade. Its numbers are declining seriously, but it is fairly common in captivity in the U.S., although there is little captive breeding.

45

INDEX

Useful Address

If you are interested in helping to save macaws, you may like to write to The National Audubon Society at the following address:

National Audubon Society
Education Division
Route 1, Box #171
Sharon, CT 06069

A Templar Book
Devised and produced by The Templar Company plc
Pippbrook Mill, London Road, Dorking
Surrey RH4 1JE, Great Britain
Copyright © 1991 by The Templar Company plc
Original text, design and illustrations copyright © 1991 by The Templar Company plc

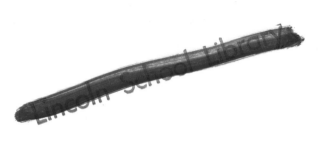